Destiny's
PURPOSE

Written by **Shannon Cassidy-Rouleau**
Illustrated by **Dennis Auth**

Publishers Cataloging-in-Publication Data

Cassidy-Rouleau, Shannon.
    Destiny's purpose / written by Shannon Cassidy-Rouleau ; illustrated
  by Dennis Auth.
        p. cm.
      Summary: An alpaca named Destiny is unable to compete in shows or
  produce fleece, but he succeeds in fulfilling another purpose.
      ISBN-13: 978-1-60131-064-4
      Includes glossary.
      [1. Alpaca—Fiction. 2. Alopecia areata—Fiction. 3. Alopecia areata—
  Juvenile fiction. 4. Farming—Juvenile fiction.] I. Auth, Dennis, ill. II. Title.
                                                    2009911224

Copyright © 2010 Shannon Cassidy-Rouleau
Printed and bound in China
First printing 2010

115 Bluebill Drive
Savannah, GA 31419
United States
(888) 300-1961

To order additional copies, please go to www.castlebridgebooks.com.

This book was published with the assistance of the helpful folks at DragonPencil.com.

For my husband, Chris, and my children, Traleena and Kieran:
you give me my purpose.

In memory of my father, who dreamed big and flew high;
and my mother, who was his safe place to land.

Special thanks to the ever-growing network of alpaca owners who have
created a community as warm and inviting as the magical animals they raise;
to Anita and "the Rouleau boys" who are always the first to lend a hand;
to my brother, John Joe, who supports my alpaca dream;
and to my Aunt Marie who nourishes my Irish roots.

The farmer and his wife squinted into the midday sun. The **alpacas** abandoned their grazing. Ears upright, necks stretched taut, the herd watched.

The newest arrival to Celtic Sunsets Ranch turned his tiny face towards the sun and closed his eyes, drinking in the warmth. As the wind blew puffs of summer breeze across the pasture, his wet fleece fluttered and began to dry. He sat upright, gangly legs tucked beneath him—the first sign that he was strong and healthy.

His knees shaking but steady, the new **cria** chanced a few wooden steps on matchstick legs. He collapsed like a marionette at Paloma's feet. She clucked against her baby's ear, nudging him to try again.

4

The farmer swelled with pride. "He sure is his mother's son, Nora. All of her offspring have been winners, and he'll be no exception! You'll see." Paloma was a prize-winning alpaca, famous in the show ring, known far and wide for her fine fleece and perfect **conformation**. "I tell you, he's destined for great things."

Nora smiled at her husband's enthusiasm. "You don't need to convince me, Peter. He's incredible." She nodded decisively. "I think we'll call him 'Destiny'."

5

As the days grew shorter, the grass yellowed and refused to grow. Outdoor feeders overflowed with fresh hay from the mow. The wind coaxed the crisp, dry leaves from every tree. They skittered over the ground and Destiny raced to catch them. His reckless jumping and quick bursts of speed caused him to collide with the **dams**. They swung their heads in his direction and threatened to **spit**.

Destiny darted quickly to safety and snuggled tightly against Paloma. He peeked bashfully from behind her legs with his "I'm-far-too-cute-to-be-mad-at" expression. When the coast was clear, he raced swiftly past the adults and **pronked** wildly across the barnyard.

Watching from the pasture, Peter shook his head and grinned. "Well, Paloma, you've sure got yourself a handful there." Opening another bag of fertilizer, he spread it slowly, taking the opportunity to check the fence for breaks and look for predator tracks. Wolves and stray dogs were always looking for a way in, and an alpaca was no match for either.

6

After the first
snowfall, Destiny
stepped cautiously onto
the fluffy white carpet, lifting
each padded foot quickly as it
disappeared into the snow.

He nosed through
the winter cover, searching
for old leaves and grass.

The farmer kept the snow cleared and the paths
sanded, but Destiny's curiosity lured him beyond the
paths. On icy ground he slipped, spun, and wobbled, like a
toy top out of control.

Peter cupped his hands to his mouth. "Destiny, come back here!" he shouted. "You'll get yourself in trouble!"

Each day, the farmer brought clean water, fresh hay, nutritious **pellets**, and sometimes a handful of barley. Destiny would trot
beside him and push his nose eagerly into the pellet feeder to steal a few of the tasty morsels.

The farmer and his wife checked their alpacas' fleece often by separating the **fibres** on each animal's side. Destiny's fleece was
thick and dense, and it shone when it was parted.

"You were right, Peter," whispered Nora eagerly. "Destiny's fleece will make beautiful **rovings** for hand spinners, and yarn for
knitters, and thread for weavers, and—"

Destiny wiggled impatiently.

"Okay, okay! Hold your horses," chuckled Peter. "Both of you will have to wait a few more months until **shearing** time."

7

While she waited, Nora thought of the plans she had for Destiny's fleece. At the winter craft shows, she pored over her knitting books, looking for ideas. Sometimes she brought her spinning wheel. As she chatted with customers, she pedaled the wheel smoothly, producing silky yarn.

Nora told everyone about the products made from alpaca fleece. "The very best fibre, around the middle," she said, "is perfect for handmade sweaters, shawls, scarves, hats, mitts, and blankets. From the **bib**, the neck, and the tops of the legs, we make cozy socks, duvets, and felted pieces."

"I've heard it's softer than wool and many times warmer," remarked a spinner, stroking a long strand of rovings.

"And it never bothers my allergies!" added one of Nora's best customers.

As spring approached, excitement grew. Nora imagined the soft yarn she would spin from Destiny's fibre. Peter pictured the approval on the judge's face when Destiny 'stole the show' at the annual alpaca competition.

The farmer threw forkfuls of yellow straw into the wagon. Days were warmer, and the alpacas no longer needed thick bedding.

He leaned against his pitchfork and looked out at the pasture. The alpacas were round-bodied and puffy—cotton balls glued upon an artist's landscape.

Destiny grazed at a leisurely pace, clipping off the new shoots with his bottom teeth. As the sun moved overhead, he rested in the shade.

When the farmer and his wife parted Destiny's fleece, the skin beneath was warm to the touch. "Good thing shearing day is close," said Peter. "A hot spring like this one is hard on the animals."

Shearing day transformed the barn into a hive of activity. Destiny pushed his way through the herd to the front of the stall. His eyes widened at the sight of the shearing and sorting tables. His ears twitched at the new voices.

Shearing was a four-person job. Nora and Peter were lucky to have the help of their neighbours. Roger was a master shearer, and Helen was skilled at trimming the teeth, the **topknots**, and the tails of the alpacas.

The cutters whined like hungry mosquitoes as they vibrated against the animals' skin. Some alpacas were quiet, some **hummed**, some spat, and some exhaled so hard that their cheeks puffed out like chipmunks storing nuts. A few even trumpeted in protest, like baby elephants.

"There, there, come on now," soothed Peter as he entered the pen to halter Destiny. Legs secured to the table, Destiny's eyes darted fearfully from Nora to Peter. The shears buzzed to life. With each pass of the clippers, Destiny's glossy caramel fleece fell away, revealing a silky summer coat. Helen gathered the buttery fleece from his **blanket** in two overflowing armfuls and placed it on the sorting table.

Destiny emerged, all legs and neck, to scamper back to the pen. The pack sniffed him as if greeting a stranger. He galloped to a nearby pile of sand to take a dirt bath. Rolling back and forth, he disappeared in a cloud of dust.

The two women chatted as they **skirted** the fleece for the mill. "I think Destiny has the finest fleece I've seen today," said Helen.

"He sure does," agreed Nora, labelling the bag and adding it to the growing pile. "It's meant for something truly exceptional!"

11

With his spectacular colouring and sweet disposition, Destiny won the admiration of visitors to the farm. At each sound of the latch, he would trot to the gate. He'd stretch his regal neck forward to give a nose-to-nose kiss, then turn and strut back to the herd.

Destiny had straight legs, a flat back, and a perfectly proportioned neck. He walked tall and carried himself like a champion. He stood calmly for toenail trims and injections. He pranced smoothly on his **lead**.

Nora and Peter knew Destiny was a winner.

"He's gonna wow 'em at the big show, Nora," said Peter.

"I think Destiny was just what this farm needed," agreed Nora.

Destiny had grown into a strong **yearling,** and it was time to separate him from his mother. Peter moved him into a field of young boys bordering the girls' pasture.

Destiny nuzzled his mother through the fence, humming plaintively to her to rescue him. But eventually he was distracted by the wonders of the field: dancing butterflies, chirping crickets, dandelion fluff, and unfurling wildflowers that tickled his nose. Before long he was off, running and playing, finding his place in his new herd.

The adult males accepted Destiny quickly. He slept safely in their midst, grazed comfortably beside them, and munched happily from their feeders.

Destiny belonged.

13

One morning, the farmer threw wide the barn doors, inviting the sun to chase away the cool night air. As the wind pushed swiftly past him, his mouth dropped open in disbelief.

Separate from the rest of the herd, Destiny lay cocooned in morning shadow. Around him were tiny mountains of champagne silk; and on his body, bare patches of pink, shiny skin. He **kushed**, head on the ground, tiny shivers rippling across his body.

14

As the farmer approached, Destiny lifted his long neck ever so slightly. He looked up at Peter with large, pleading eyes. Slowly, the rest of the herd stood and, without a backward glance, left Destiny alone.

The farmer sprinted towards the house. "Nora," he yelled, "call the vet! There's something wrong with Destiny!"

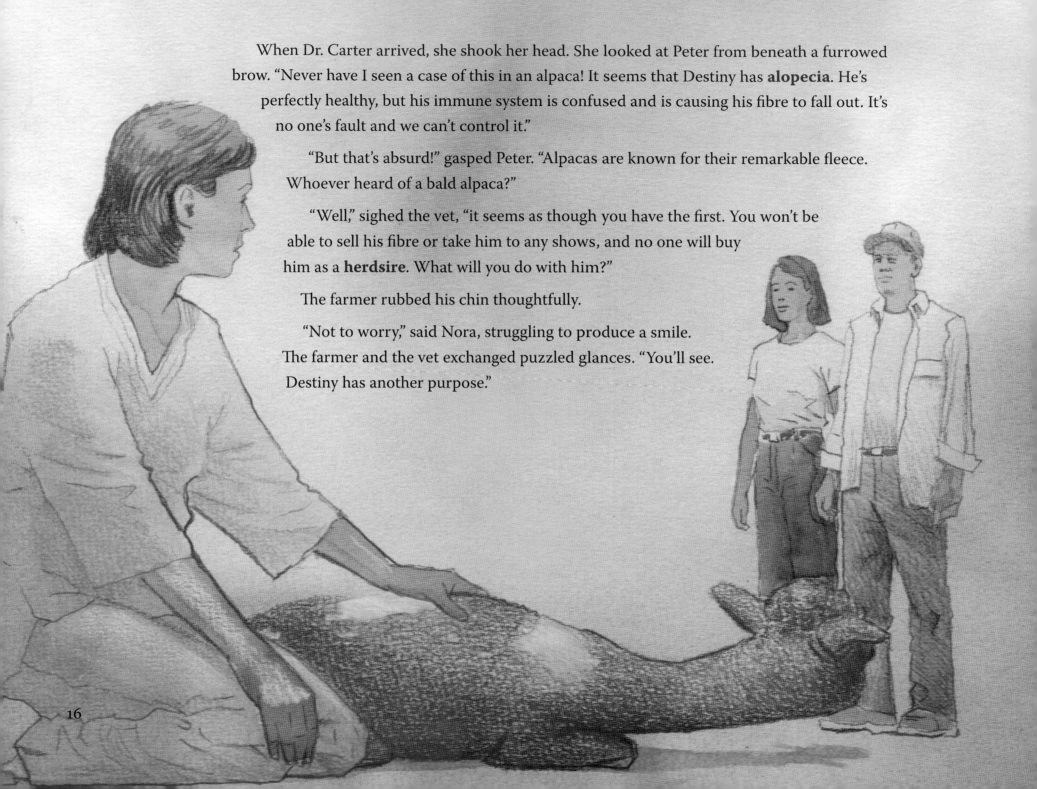

When Dr. Carter arrived, she shook her head. She looked at Peter from beneath a furrowed brow. "Never have I seen a case of this in an alpaca! It seems that Destiny has **alopecia**. He's perfectly healthy, but his immune system is confused and is causing his fibre to fall out. It's no one's fault and we can't control it."

"But that's absurd!" gasped Peter. "Alpacas are known for their remarkable fleece. Whoever heard of a bald alpaca?"

"Well," sighed the vet, "it seems as though you have the first. You won't be able to sell his fibre or take him to any shows, and no one will buy him as a **herdsire**. What will you do with him?"

The farmer rubbed his chin thoughtfully.

"Not to worry," said Nora, struggling to produce a smile. The farmer and the vet exchanged puzzled glances. "You'll see. Destiny has another purpose."

16

Each day, Peter noticed the changes.

As he shovelled the day's waste into the wheelbarrow, Destiny didn't nibble mischievously at his coat. As he filled the water trough, Destiny didn't splash playfully in the clean water. As he poured the **mineral** mix into the feeder, Destiny didn't dip his nose into the fine powder.

The other males lifted their heads in the air when Destiny approached and made warning sounds in their throats. If he didn't pay attention, they covered him with grassy spit that made him squeeze his eyes shut and turn away.

He slept on the outskirts of the herd, he grazed separately from his mates, and he ate last at the hay feeder. Destiny's head hung low; he didn't walk straight-necked and flat-backed. His powder puff tail did not flick proudly, and he no longer greeted visitors at the gate.

Destiny was an outcast.

Just after sunup on the day of the big show, the farmer and his wife loaded their three best alpacas into the trailer. The rest of the herd chased the trailer as far as the fence allowed. The farmer looked back. Destiny was alone in the barnyard.

"I was certain we'd be taking Destiny to this show," said Peter, turning his gaze to the road. "He was sure to win."

"A ribbon isn't the only measure of worth. You'll see," Nora nodded. "Destiny has another purpose."

18

The show barn was abuzz with anticipation. **Handlers** walked briskly between the barn and the show ring. Alpacas hummed nervously inside their pens. Judges observed competing alpacas in the ring, checking their teeth and examining their fleece on the display table. Spectators filled the bleachers, and old farm friends caught up on news from nearby ranches.

As they drove home, Nora ran her fingers over a bright red ribbon. "Nellie looked like a champ in the ring. This will show people that she's a great alpaca."

"Sure, it's a nice ribbon," said Peter half-heartedly. "But maybe alpacas are worth more than the ribbons they win."

Nora looked out the window and smiled.

As the sun fell towards the horizon, Peter hung the final halter on its hook. He added the shiny ribbon to the others on the prize wall. The excitement of the show was over, and the alpacas grazed contentedly. They would sleep well tonight.

He walked slowly to the house, his shoulders slumped, his steps sluggish.

On the porch, Nora glanced up from her knitting. She nodded to the chair beside her, inviting him to sit. Peter's rocker moved in time to the click-clack cadence of his wife's knitting needles. The yarn slid swiftly through her fingers, silent and sure.

"That's the yarn from Destiny's fibre, isn't it?" asked Peter, reaching out to feel its softness. "That looks a little long for a sweater."

"It's just right," said Nora. "You'll see when it's done."

Peter watched Destiny, separate and small, grazing at the edge of the field beneath the old willow. "I'm worried," he murmured. "Destiny is alone. Alpacas are herd animals. They need each other. What will become of him?"

"Not to worry. You'll see," soothed his wife, the butterscotch yarn flying over the needles. "Destiny has another purpose."

21

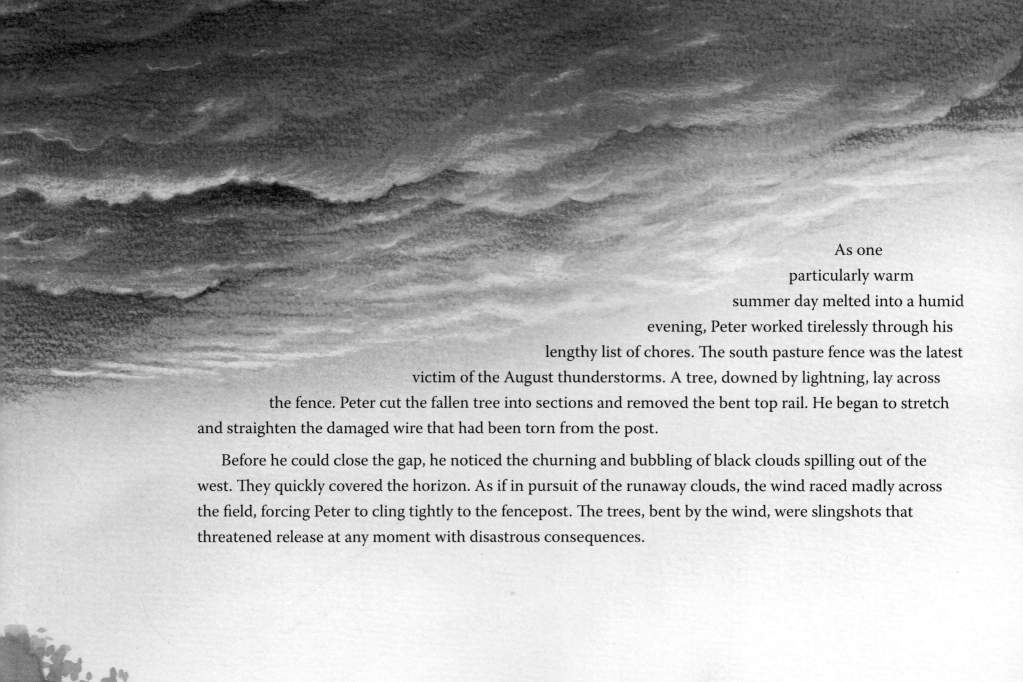

As one
particularly warm
summer day melted into a humid
evening, Peter worked tirelessly through his
lengthy list of chores. The south pasture fence was the latest
victim of the August thunderstorms. A tree, downed by lightning, lay across
the fence. Peter cut the fallen tree into sections and removed the bent top rail. He began to stretch
and straighten the damaged wire that had been torn from the post.

Before he could close the gap, he noticed the churning and bubbling of black clouds spilling out of the west. They quickly covered the horizon. As if in pursuit of the runaway clouds, the wind raced madly across the field, forcing Peter to cling tightly to the fencepost. The trees, bent by the wind, were slingshots that threatened release at any moment with disastrous consequences.

Without warning, thunderous gongs boomed from the blackened sky. Peter clenched his teeth as torrents of cold, wet rain pelted him without pardon.

Finally, he released his grip on the post. He staggered headlong into the wind, bracing himself as he pushed towards the farmhouse. He squeezed inside as a crooked white finger stabbed sharply through the angry clouds.

"I couldn't finish the fence," he called breathlessly to his wife, "but the alpacas won't venture out in the storm. They'll be safe in the barn tonight."

The storm howled long after the farmhouse lights had dimmed. The alpacas clamoured to find shelter away from the whipping wind. The barn doors had blown apart and they flapped frantically back and forth.

The herd huddled in a corner of the barn. Destiny kushed alone. He pulled his legs tightly under his body to stay warm against the driving rain.

At first the alpacas sensed, rather than saw, the shadowy forms circling the barn. They flattened their ears against their heads and raised their noses into the wind. Something was not right.

Illuminated by the moon, three sinister figures took shape: glowing eyes, gleaming teeth, guttural snarls—grey wolves.

The alpacas scattered. They backed
away, spit into the night air, and jostled,
like evacuees at a fire drill, to get to
the back of the barn. With no escape,
they watched helplessly as the wolves
approached.

Abruptly, Destiny bolted upright, filling
the open space between the wolves and the herd.
He stood tall, his head erect, his stare defiant. The
storm quieted. The only sound piercing the night air
was the shrill **alarm call** of a single alpaca.

The farmer and his wife jumped
from their bed. They exchanged panicked glances while scrambling to dress. Grabbing flashlights, the
nervous pair plunged into the dark night. They approached the barn just in time to see three silver tails
disappearing out of the flashlight's reach and bounding beyond the open fence line.

Peter and Nora surveyed the damage. The animals, restless and anxious, drew closer to the alpaca at
the forefront. They dropped their necks and heads to him and lowered their gaze.

Destiny met the farmer's surprised stare with strong, dark eyes.

Each day, Peter noticed the changes.

Destiny slept in the centre of the barn, surrounded by his herd. He grazed alongside his mates and ate first at the hay feeder. When a weaker alpaca, a new arrival, or one less than perfect joined the group, Destiny drew him a little closer, grazed with him a little longer, and invited him to the feeder a little sooner.

Destiny had a purpose.

Two young cria
bounced across the
pasture, chasing the crumpled
leaves that swirled in tiny circles.

"I think it's a perfect fit," said Peter. Despite the autumn breeze, Destiny didn't shiver in his new coat. His fibre *had* been meant for something truly extraordinary: lovingly spun, carefully knit, and returned to keep him warm.

"You know, his fleece could grow back someday," Nora pointed out.

"If it does, that will be great," said Peter. He paused. "If it doesn't, that will be okay too."

28

"Now I *know* that Destiny was just what this farm needed," said Nora.

"You know, it's like I always said," mused Peter. "You didn't need to worry. Destiny had another purpose."

Nora looked up quickly, in time to see the corners of her husband's lips curve ever so slightly into a sheepish grin. She raised her hand to shield her eyes from the sun, and as the breeze playfully tousled her hair, Nora smiled.

29

ALPACAS are members of the camelid family. They are native to South America. Alpacas are herd animals and need the company of other alpacas to be happy.

Alpacas are gentle animals. They communicate through body language and by humming softly. They rarely spit at people, but do spit at each other over food or when they are upset.

There are two types of alpacas: huacaya (wuh-*ki*-ah), with tight, crimped fibre; and suri (sir-*ee),* with long, shiny fibre that hangs to the ground.

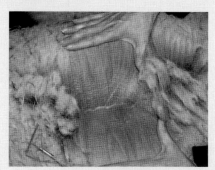

CHECKING FLEECE

The name for alpaca fleece is fibre. Alpacas are sheared once each year to harvest the fibre and keep the alpaca cool in the summer months. The fibre comes in twenty-two natural colours and can be spun into yarn, used for duvets, or felted. The fibre is warmer than wool and does not cause itching.

The female alpaca is called a hembra. The male alpaca is called a macho. Mothers carry their babies for more than eleven months. A baby alpaca is called a cria. Usually only one cria is born at a time.

Alpacas are cared for by their owners and by veterinarians. They require shots to prevent disease and their toenails need to be trimmed every few months. Alpacas only have teeth in their lower jaws. Some alpacas need to have their teeth trimmed to keep them working well.

Alpacas enjoy hay and grass and require fresh water each day. Their food travels through three stomach compartments, and they chew their cud. Alpacas receive a pellet or mixed supplement to be sure that they get all of the nutrients they need. Some farmers also give their alpacas a powdered mineral mixture.

Most alpaca farmers are also breeders and raise their alpacas to be sold to others interested in owning these animals. Some alpacas go to shows where they may

BEFORE SHEARING

AFTER SHEARING

FLEECE ON THE SKIRTING TABLE

win ribbons. Sometimes only the alpaca's fleece is sent to a show to be judged.

Alpacas use an alarm call to warn their herd of possible danger. Their only defences are to spit or to run, so alpacas need good fences to keep predators out.

A ROLL IN THE DIRT

Alpacas do well on small properties. Although they are hardy, they do require adequate shelter to protect them from harsh weather. With a lifespan of up to twenty years, alpacas bring many years of joy to the farmers who raise them.

For more information, visit **www.alpacainfo.com**.

About Alopecia

ALOPECIA AREATA (al-oh-pee-sheeah air-ee-ah-tah) is a disease that causes the hair to fall out. It is not contagious.

There are different types of alopecia. *Alopecia areata* is the name used to describe patchy hair loss anywhere on the body. *Alopecia totalis* is the term used when all of the scalp hair is lost. It is called *alopecia universalis* when the hair is lost from the entire scalp and body.

Some form of alopecia is experienced by 1.7% of all people. For most of them, it happens before the age of twenty.

Alopecia is an autoimmune condition. Something triggers the immune system to see the hair follicle as an enemy and attack it. The hair falls out and stops growing. Doctors don't know if the trigger comes from inside the body or outside the body.

Alopecia is unpredictable. For many, the hair re-grows but may fall out again without warning. For other sufferers, the hair never grows back.

There is no cure for alopecia areata. Doctors can try medications that alter the body's immune system. There are some treatments that can be injected into the scalp, taken in pill form, or rubbed on the scalp. Some people with alopecia wear wigs.

Alopecia sufferers are usually very healthy. Their hair loss does not hurt or make them feel ill. But, alopecia causes a lot of emotional pain. People with alopecia can lose their self-esteem. Having no control over their bodies can make them fearful and worried. Children with alopecia may be teased or bullied. Adults with alopecia are afraid of what other people may think or say.

Organizations such as the National Alopecia Areata Foundation raise money for research to find a cure, and offer information and support to people suffering from this disease.

For more information, visit **www.naaf.org**.